JOSEPH BUSA

ALSO BY JOSEPH BUSA

Data Harvester

Grendel and the Masters of the Universe

The Key to the Pit: Resurrection

A Tale from Ripper Street: Inspector Edmund Reid's Hunt for Jack the Ripper

Wellcome to Hell: Was Sir Henry Wellcome Jack the Ripper?

JOSEPH BUSA

Business Secrets of the Pharaohs: Exodus to Brexodus

JOSEPH BUSA

ISBN-13: 978-1725674929
ISBN-10: 1725674920

To Michelle

CHAPTER ONE

Merkha and Thethi were nearly at their wit's end. In recent months they'd witnessed nine plagues comprising: Blood, Frogs, Gnats, Flies, Livestock, Boils, Hail, Locusts and Darkness. Their trusty Israelite slave had warned them to expect a tenth plague starting in the middle of the night. They were sat, beakers of date beer in hand, worrying and waiting.

'Are you sure that this tenth plague of Moses's is going to kick-off tonight, Thoth?' asked a slightly pissed Merkha.

'Yes, master. All Israelite slaves have been warned that the Lord will pass over our homes tonight,' replied Thoth.

'The lads at the counting house say that your man Moses is a fraud. Word has it that every one of his plagues has been replicated by Pharaoh's magicians.'

'If they can replicate them, why haven't they been able to reverse them?' replied Thoth.

'I don't know, I'm just telling you what I've heard.'

'And what about you, master Thethi? Does the priesthood have an opinion?'

'You know full well that I'm persona non grata in the gods' temples.'

'That hasn't stopped you stealing your fill of food and pomegranate wine with your fake junior priest ID of yours,' said Merkha.

'It's alright for you to be so high and mighty, Mr junior scribe. With your guaranteed income and all,' said Thethi.

'Well at least I'm out there trying to earn a living. Anyway, enough of all that. Thoth!'

'Yes, master.'

'Tell me again. Why was it necessary for you to burn the remains of our lamb meal? And what's with all the blood you daubed over the doorway? There are flies everywhere.'

'As I explained to you. Word in the market is that the

Lord will pass over each and every house in the EU this night.'

'And why is that bad again?'

'I already told you. I don't know. All I know is that all the slaves have killed and eaten a lamb this day and daubed the animal's blood over their doorways.'

'But this is my home not yours. How's this god of yours going to know the difference?'

'How the Lord knows is irrelevant. What matters is that you slaughtered a year old lamb without defect and I daubed its blood over the doorframe.'

'And burnt all leftovers!'

'I'm sorry, master, that was what the elders have instructed us to do.'

'So, we're safe from your magician Moses's latest illusion?'

'With all due respect, master, how can one consider the nine plagues the work of a magician?'

'You're right, as usual, Thoth. Take no notice of Merkha, he's drunk,' said an equally drunk Thethi.

'Well I'm fed-up waiting. Thoth, I order you to tell us what you're trying to protect us from!' shouted Merkha.

'I'm sorry, master, I cannot. I was warned to take precautions, but from what I do not know.'

'You're lucky that I believe you, else I'd have beaten it out of you,' said Merkha, to which Thoth responded by raising his eyebrows. His master had threatened to beat him on several occasions in recent years, but never had, and Thoth didn't imagine that he'd be on the receiving end of a punishment beating anytime soon. 'Don't be looking like that, I mean it. There are two of us. We'd soon get the better of you.'

'Then beat away, master, I can only reiterate what I have told you.'

'Don't think I'm bluffing, Thoth, I could always call-in one of the Slave Drivers. You know better than I that those Neanderthals will beat you for the fun of it.'

'As you wish, master Merkha.'

'You're spoilt you know. You hardly do a stroke and as for my allowing you to name yourself after one of our most revered gods! It's blasphemy you know. I could get into a hell of a lot of trouble over something like -' Suddenly the candles flickered and a cold chill passed through the reed house. 'Did you feel that?' asked Merkha.

'It has begun, master,' said Thoth.

It was a few minutes before the screaming began. It took a while for Merkha and Thethi to understand what was happening. It seemed that every firstborn child and animal belonging to an Egyptian had died suddenly in its sleep. The two men continued to drink date beer until the early hours, when they finally collapsed into unconsciousness. It was the only way anyone would sleep that night.

CHAPTER TWO

No one, not even the Pharaoh, had escaped what Moses was calling the Lord's wrath. As the Pharaoh, Khufu, had stared at the lifeless body of his son his first thought had been for vengeance, but those feelings soon turned to fear. Fear, not for himself but for the rest of his family.

His advisors had pleaded with him to have Moses, Moses's brother Aaron and all the elders of the Israelites executed. But Khufu didn't act in haste, he waited, seeking a means of dealing with the Israelite slaves that would not pit him against the will of their god. Khufu had been told from birth that he was a god incarnate, but at times he felt like a mere mortal. He was the Guardian of Maat and knew that his worthiness to enter the next world depended on how he responded to the tenth, and hopefully last, of the Israelite plagues. He had learnt nothing from his visit to the oracle of Ipet-isu, but took that to mean that he should wait before making a final decision on how to respond to the demands of Moses and the elders.

Khufu's patience was rewarded. A drunken junior priest had been overheard blaspheming outside the grounds of the palace. The Pharaoh had been told that the man had dared suggest that he knew how to resolve the problem that clearly the Pharaoh wasn't capable of solving on his own. Ordinarily, the man would have been executed on the spot, but under the circumstances the senior priests decided to have the man beaten before bringing the matter to the attention of the Pharaoh, so that he might be held solely responsible for the man's fate.

'Rise!' commanded Khufu as he tried to determine the quality of the man sprawled out in front of him. The man had professed to be a junior priest, yet dressed like a peasant. Nothing about the man's being suggested how he had managed to find himself in the presence of the

Pharaoh.

Thethi's hands were tied behind his back and he was in a lot of pain, but none of his bones had been broken, so he was able to rise to his feet unaided.

'Tell me the solution to the slave problem that I, Pharaoh, am incapable of formulating without your console!' demanded Khufu.

'Please forgive me, Great One, I have spoken out of turn,' said a bewildered, battered and dehydrated Thethi.

'Tell me the solution or die. The choice is yours to make,' said Khufu, being careful to ensure that the fates would be held responsible for the mans and possibly the Egyptian nation's future.

'All I said was that the Israelites might be granted a *Referendum* to determine their fate.'

'Referendum? I have not heard this word before. Explain its meaning to me,' said the Pharaoh in a slightly less assured tone. He had been taught to believe that all words had their own innate power. For a low born man to utter a word he had not heard before made Khufu think that the man might actually be a messenger from the gods.

'What I mean is that you could allow the slaves to vote on their future.'

'Explain!' commanded Khufu, his face forming the faintest of smiles.

'Our lazy slaves are obviously keen to follow Moses when he suggests their spending a few weeks in the desert avoiding backbreaking labour. Who wouldn't? But what if you gave them a choice of total freedom? I don't mean freedom to live as free men, sharing Egypt's comforts, I mean freedom to leave Egypt and return to their homeland of Judea?'

'Explain!' demanded Khufu, his expression returning to a mask of stone.

'Why not give them a vote to determine whether they stay here in Egypt as slaves or leave our land forever? The freedom to live without roofs over their heads, without the guarantee of food and water, without the security of Pharaoh's great army to protect them?'

Khufu's expression softened again. Yes he thought, this low born man had truly relayed a solution from the gods. The Israelite slaves would determine their own fate and he, Pharaoh, would be free from the wrath of their god, safe in the knowledge that the majority of slaves could be trusted not to vote for total freedom. Few, other than the zealots, would relish the possibility of wandering the arid deserts forever.

'What is your name, priest?' asked Khufu.

'Thethi.'

'You, Thethi, are clearly a man of great wisdom. From this day forth you and your family will move into a house within the grounds of the palace. In return for the honour I bestow upon you, you will be required to sit and debate with the senior priests on matters of state.'

'Thank you, Pharaoh,' said Thethi as the guards untied the knots binding his hands behind his back.

'I have one last question before you are free to leave my presence … What question should the slaves be instructed to vote for?'

'Something along the lines of "Should the people of Judea remain slaves within the Egyptian Union or should they leave the Egyptian Union?". You know, something, simple that won't allow for any misunderstanding or confusion after the event.'

'You may leave,' said Khufu, and the guards escorted Thethi out of the great hall.

CHAPTER THREE

Thoth walked into the reed house carrying two large wicker baskets and placed them next to a pile of clothes he had stacked neatly on a mat.

'What are you doing?' asked Merkha.

'Packing, master.'

'I can see that. But who told you to?'

'I dreamt last night that we are about to embark on a journey.'

'A dream! Have you gone mad? Is this the start of Moses's next plague? Your insubordination increases by the day. This won't do you know.'

'Master, there is something that I must tell you.'

'What is it? Come on, spit it out, man!'

'There was talk in the market.'

'Talk?'

'I heard a rumour that Thethi has been arrested.'

'What? What for? He hasn't been on the pomegranate wine again, has he? He'll never learn.'

'Supposedly he was arrested and escorted into the grounds of the palace by the Pharaonic Guard under orders of a senior priest.'

'What? Why didn't you tell me this earlier?'

'It is only a rumour, I don't know if it is true or not. But if it is, my dream foretold -'

'Forgot about your bloody dream. Thethi should have been back ages ago. Senior priest! The Pharaonic guard! This is bloody serious. I told him to stop impersonating a junior priest. I bet the idiot was stupid enough to present his fake credentials to one of the palace priests. Any fool can see that the seal on that stone tablet of his is a forgery. I'm a junior scribe, they are bound to accuse me of forging the thing for him. Bloody hell, what are we going to do?'

'I don't wish to disturb you unnecessarily, master, but a

contingent of the Pharaonic Guard are marching this way.'

'What? I'll bet the idiot used one of my seals. We need to destroy them, listen you -'

'Open up under order of the Pharaonic Guard!' came a shout from outside of the front door.

Before Merkha had time to move, the door was forced open and two huge men entered the reed house followed by a very senior looking priest.

'Are you the one called, Merkha?' asked Pawah, Pharaoh's High Priest.

'Yes,' replied Merkha. 'Listen, I didn't do anything wrong. Everything he told you is a lie. I had nothing to do with –'

'Nothing to do with what?' asked Thethi as he entered the reed house.

'What? Oh, nothing,' replied Merkha staring at bruises on Thethi's face. 'What's going on, Thethi?'

'You are to come with us,' said Pawah.

'Where are we going, Thethi?'

'We're moving into the palace grounds.'

'What? Why? How?'

'You're the closest thing I have to family. I thought you might like to swap this reed hovel of yours for a limestone brick house and a life of luxury within the walls of the palace. However, nobody's forcing you to move. You are free to stay here if you really want to.'

'No, no. A life of luxury you say? Within the walls of the palace. What exactly would I have to do for that?'

'Absolutely nothing. 'Don't worry about it, I'll explain everything later on,' said Thethi before turning to Thoth. 'Slave, start packing-up our belongings and be quick about it!'

Thethi had been careful not to call Thoth by his name. He knew there'd be hell to pay if Pharaoh's High Priest learnt that he and Merkha addressed their slave by the name of a god.

Thoth nodded and immediately returned to the task he'd been performing before Thethi's arrival.

'Were you were expecting us, slave?' asked Pawah, eyeing Thoth suspiciously.

'No, master. I was merely tidying-up my master's belongings.'

'I see,' said Pawah continuing to study Thoth. 'Show me your hands, slave.'

Thoth held his hands out so that Pawah could see them. 'You don't have the hands of a slave. It is clear that your masters have been too lenient with you. It is custom that only slaves born within the walls of the palace may set foot inside there. However, for you, slave, I will make an exception. What is your name?'

'I named the slave, Ineni,' said Merkha quickly, not allowing Thoth time to answer.

'An architect is a lofty title for a slave,' said Pawah. 'Are you are an Israelite by birth?'

'Yes,' replied Thoth.

'Remove your robe, slave.'

'What?'

'Don't make me repeat my command.'

Thoth removed his robe and was stood stark naked in the middle of the room.

'Your foreskin is intact. Isn't it custom for all Israelite men to be circumcised?'

'Yes it is,' replied Thoth.

'You are the most unusual of slaves are you not?'

'I don't understand your question, master.'

'Cover yourself up again. What does the word *Referendum* mean to you, Merkha?' asked Pawah, directing his question to Merkha whilst continuing to fix his gaze upon the slave, Thoth.

'I am sorry, but I have never heard that word before. What does it mean?' replied Merkha.

'And what about you, slave, have you heard this word

before?'

'I am but an ignorant slave, such talk is lost on me, master.'

'And your name, slave. Remind me, what was it again?'

Thoth paused before answering and a palpable tension started to fill the room.

'It's Ineni, master.'

'Oh yes, Ineni, that was most forgetful of me. Get back to your work, Ineni, you still have much to do. Re's barge will soon have sailed its course for the day. The guards will escort you to the palace when you have finished.'

CHAPTER FOUR

'What the hell have you done, Thethi?' asked Merkha after the High Priest and his Pharaonic Guards had finally left them to their own devices.

'I'm sorry. One minute my fake junior priest ID had help wangle me a large offering of pomegranate wine, the next, I found myself spouting-off about how I could solve the slave problem. I think one of the senior priests or their spies overheard me.'

'You're a bloody idiot, but then you already know that. What are those for?' said Merkha pointing at a room he thought might be a temple.

'The large raised surface is called a table and the smaller things around it are called chairs,' said Thethi.

'Are they used to worship the gods?'

'No, they are used for eating meals. Pawah told me that within the walls of the Royal palaces, the only people who eat from mats laid over the floor are slaves.'

'Are you sure about that? I mean, the last thing we want is for somebody to accuse us of disrespecting the gods.'

'Don't worry about it. I'm absolutely certain that's what they are used for.'

'Okay then, back to this big idea of yours. Explain it to me.'

'Well I seem to have invented something I've named a Referendum.'

'Well, what the hell is one and how do they work?'

'It's pretty simple really. You use it to give people a vote on their own futures.'

'You do what?'

'Give people, by that I mean slaves, a –'

'I bloody heard you the first time. Why they didn't put you straight to death is beyond me. Whatever you do, don't go mentioning any of that rubbish in earshot of the Vizier or you'll be killed where you stand.'

'Don't worry about the Vizier, I've already explained my invention to the Pharaoh.'

'What? You've spoken with the Pharaoh?'

'As hard as it might be to believe. Yes I have.'

'And you persuaded Pharaoh to give the slaves a vote on their own future?'

'Yes.'

'What the hell are they going to be voting on?'

'This is the beauty of my idea. Pharaoh is going to grant them an in/out vote on whether they want to remain as slaves within the EU.'

'That's your idea?'

'Yes. Can't you see how brilliant it is?'

'No I bloody well can't.'

'Listen, it's easy. The Israelites get to vote on whether to remain slaves within the EU, with all the benefits that come with living within the borders of the world's most powerful trading nation, or to up sticks and leave. Who, apart from Moses, will want the freedom to wander the desert lands without the guarantee of security, food or water? You can imagine the reception six hundred thousand of the downtrodden will receive when they try to cross a border back into the land of Judea or worse, the border of one of our enemies.'

'What makes you so sure that they won't be welcomed back to their old homeland with open arms?'

'We allowed Moses back home and look what disruption he's caused, and there's only one of him!'

'Yes, I see your point. And you came up with this Referendum idea all on your own?'

'Well not exactly. I think I was only repeating what I overheard someone else saying.'

'Who do you know who could have thought-up an idea like that?'

'I can't actually think of anybody I know who's that

clever.'

'Well thanks very much for your vote of confidence, friend.'

'I meant anyone other than your good self of course.'
And if he believes that he'll believe anything.

'Well, it's your idea now and we're going to bloody well make sure that nobody takes it away from you. At least not whilst we are living the highlife within the walls of the palatial grounds.'

CHAPTER FIVE

A week had passed since Pharaoh granted the Israelite slaves their referendum. As Thethi had predicted, gossip overheard in the marketplaces indicated that the slaves knew what was good for them and were going to vote to remain in the EU. Of course, carefully planted stories of attacks on caravan trains and the death and slaughter of families who'd foolishly tried, and failed, to cross the deserts were helping to shape the slaves' voting intentions.

For the first time in months Khufu felt sufficiently relaxed to get a full night's sleep. He was feeling evermore confident his referendum was truly an act that would appease the Israelite god. But all that was about to change.

Pawah, the High Priest, wouldn't allow Thethi out of the palace grounds without an armed escort, but Merkha was free to come and go as he pleased. And it was on one such excursion that he found himself face-to-face with a camel being paraded through a market to the beating of drums. The spectacle caught his and everyone else in the market's attention.

Most slaves were barely literate, but the all seemed to be able to read the carefully painted slogan daubed in large letters onto the leather hides draped over the sides of the camel. The words, painted in red okra dye, read:

Vote Leave – For a Land of Milk and Honey

Milk and honey! The only place they'll find any of that is inside the grounds of the palace and I won't be giving them any of mine, thought Merkha. Then the junior scribe in him took over and he started to study the brushstrokes that formed the words. *The fool wouldn't have been stupid enough to write that, would he?* But Merkha knew full well that the slogan was exactly the kind of thing Thethi might write.

When Merkha returned back to the opulence of the palace grounds and his limestone brick home, he found Thethi fast asleep on a chaise longue.

'Wake-up you fool!'

'What? What's happening?' asked a bleary-eyed Thethi.

'What the hell's gotten into you?'

'I don't know what you're talking about.'

'So you don't know anything about the slogan being paraded through the street markets on the side of a camel?'

'A slogan of the side of a camel?'

'Yes.'

'Saying what exactly?'

'Saying that voting leave, is a vote for a land of milk and honey.'

Thethi burst out laughing. 'And what makes you think that I would have had anything to do that?'

'Let me see,' said Merkha. 'Could it be that the words were painted in a style matching your own handwriting or might it be that the shade of okra used exactly matches the stains on your fingers?'

Thethi looked down at his hands and winced. 'You got me.'

'I don't know what's gotten into you. Have you developed a death wish or something?'

'You need to lighten up. It was only a bit of harmless fun.'

'Well your bit of harmless fun seemed to be creating quite a stir in the marketplace!'

'Please, try to keep your voice down.'

'Yes, you're right, for a change. Pawah's spies are everywhere.'

'I didn't mean that. I've got a blinding headache.'

'You've been on the pomegranate wine again, haven't you?'

'What if I have?'

'You know you can't take the stuff. Most every time you drink it you end up doing the stupidest of things. Couldn't you go back to drinking date beer, at least until this bloody referendum is over and done with? We're onto a good thing here and I don't want you ruining it for us.'

'Okay, I promise. No more pomegranate wine until after the result of the referendum. You know your problem, you worry too much. Most slaves can't read and those that can are never going to fall for slogan promising them milk and honey. It was only a bit of fun.'

'We are living in the strangest of times. I mean, I still don't believe that you've actually spoken to the Pharaoh. Who knows what your little stunt might lead to?'

'I need another drink. I reckon you should have one with me.'

'By the looks of you, you've had more than enough already.'

'Get some date beer down your neck and stop worrying.'

'I would do, but where's that workshy slave of ours gone?'

'Oh! I might have ordered him not to return until he's paraded that camel through every marketplace in Memphis.'

'And what if he gets arrested? We won't be able to disown him. Everyone, including the High Priest, knows that he belongs to us.'

'You mean, belongs to you.'

'What?'

'He's not my slave. You're the fool that bought him.'

Just then Thoth entered the house.

'Where the hell have you been?' demanded Merkha.

'Master Thethi ordered me to walk our camel through every marketplace in Memphis.'

'You should have finished that hours ago,' said Thethi.

'You are correct, master, but I'm afraid that the camel was stolen from me.'

'Stolen!' shouted Merkha not wanting to believe his ears. 'Then again, maybe that's a good thing. At least this won't come back to our door should the priests get involved again.'

'A mob under the control of the elders took it from me.'

'What? The elders have my camel?'

'I tried, master. But they beat me and caste me out into the desert.'

'Do you know where they went with it?'

'My guess would be, Thebes.'

'That's miles away. What makes you think they were going to take it there?'

'I overheard them talking about parading it outside the Pharaoh's other centre of power.'

'Okay, forget about it. It might even prove to be a blessing in disguise. The way I see it, the father away the thing is from us the better.'

CHAPTER SIX

On the night before the referendum there were massive thunder storms across Egypt. The portents weren't good and Pharaoh Khufu was worried about the outcome. In spite of every scare story his officials could muster, intelligence gathered from conversations overheard in the markets indicated that there was chance that the slaves might actually vote to leave. The Pharaoh's closest advisers had urged him to tamper with the results, but Khufu would have none of it. He considered the whole business to be a trial by the gods and he wasn't going to do anything to jeopardize his own immortality. Khufu had risked all on the strength of a free vote, and lost – once the results had been counted it was revealed that the slaves had voted to leave by the slenderest of majorities.

The results known, Khufu called an urgent meeting with viziers of every conurbation, all of whom were eager to find a scapegoat to explain the results. After many hours of discussion, Pawah, the High Priest, rose to speak.

'I have listened to the consul given to our esteemed Pharaoh, but sadly I feel that you all miss the point. We have four issues to focus upon. Firstly, the Pharaoh must be seen to grant the slaves their wish. They must be allowed to pack-up and leave without harassment. Secondly, a pretext must be found for invalidating the vote. Some issue must be found to split the leavers, my suggestion is the land border separating the two Egypts from Libya. We must exaggerate problems with supplying our military garrison there, prompting fears over the future security of the Western Front. Thirdly, all attacks on travellers in the deserts must be attributed to the Bedouin Sand-dwellers, regardless of who the perpetrators really are. Our intelligence indicates that the slaves are afraid of the Sandpeople, we must do more to play on their fears. Lastly, an investigation must be mounted to identify the person or persons behind the tactics adopted by the Vote Leave campaign. We must rubbish them, linking their campaign to extremist elements within our society. It may only have been a simple slogan paraded on the side of a camel, but I sense that a pernicious intellect was responsible for it. If we are lucky, we might yet force a second a vote.'

'You really think this possible, Pawah?' asked Khufu.

'Yes, Your Highness. People are fickle and tend not to like change. The slaves might not have the best of lives, but they are guaranteed food, shelter and security. Only a fool would readily give that up on the promise of a land of milk and honey.'

'The false priest, Thethi, what of him?'

'He is free to roam the palace grounds, but we monitor his movement at all times.'

'Have you found anything linking him to the campaign waged by Moses and the elders?'

'There are rumours, but we no direct evidence of it. I fear that he is but a useful idiot, one of many pawns being moved by the aforesaid unknown pernicious intellect, Your Highness.'

'I was told he has no family and that his only connection to the masses is the companion he shares a home with and that slave of theirs.'

'Yes, Your Highness. My feeling is that one or both are driving his actions.'

'You suggest that a junior scribe and/or a slave are responsible for this debacle?'

Pawah's mouth went dry and he had difficulty speaking. 'Do not the gods work in mysterious ways, your Highness?'

'You dare question me?' said the Pharaoh his expression hardening. The tone of his words caused the guards to stand ready for action.

Pawah swallowed a few times trying desperately to wet the back of his throat. 'No, Your Highness, never. I was merely making a statement.'

'Invite all three of them to dine with me tomorrow evening. It will be revealed to me whether any of them are truly in contact with the gods.'

'Yes, Your Highness.'

'And one last thing … you, Pawah, are also invited to join us.'

'Thank you, Your Highness.'

CHAPTER SEVEN

Merkha looked like a condemned man. Nobody would have guessed that he had just been informed that he had been invited to attend one of the most prestigious events in the life of an Egyptian, breaking bread with the Pharaoh.

'I don't want to go!' shouted Merkha.

'I don't know what you're worrying about. If you think we've been eating well since we moved into the palace grounds, you wait and see what they'll serve-up tomorrow night.'

'Yes, great. We'll have our fill of sumptuous delicacies, right up until the point where members of the Pharaonic Guard start beating us to death with their maces.'

'Stop being so ridiculous. You really think that the Pharaoh would invite us to diner if he intended to have us tortured and killed? Why would he bother?'

'I suppose you're right.'

'I know I'm right.'

'But we lost that bloody referendum of yours. He can't be happy that most of our slaves are going to be set free. I mean, who's going to do all their work? What do you think, Thoth? You've been very quiet on the matter or have you been holding your tongue until you're officially made a free man?'

'I think that dining with Pharaoh will be the most interesting of experiences, and I'm looking forward to it,' said Thoth. 'Who knows, maybe Pharaoh would like to hear your views on how to restructure the economy following the *Exodus*.'

'The what?' asked Merkha.

'The Exodus. That's what they are calling our forthcoming migration into the desert lands. Master Merkha, aren't you always commenting on how you'd make a better job of running the Union than Pharaoh's administrators? Well tomorrow night you'll be able to explain your ideas to an audience with the power to make a difference.'

'Actually, you might just have a point. You slaves leaving us is going to give us all sorts of issues to deal with.'

'Not least of which is who is going to serve the date beer,' said Thethi waving an empty beaker over his head.

'The way I see it, the main question is whether we replace Thoth and his pals with slaves from another land?'

'Now you're thinking, master. And what of the border with Libya?'

'What of it?'

'Don't you have an open border with Libya because of the Egyptian garrison stationed on their land?'

'Everyone knows about the open border. What of it?'

'The Israelite slaves will be given their freedom there as well as in the Union. Might the soldiers' families want to return home once they have no one to support them? And what of trade with the Nubians in the south? How might that be effected? Won't this give them a trading advantage over you?'

'You know what, Thoth, this might just be the opportunity I've been looking for. Yes, I've been telling you two all about the limitations of the Pharaoh's ingots and coins for years and where has it gotten me? Nowhere. Now, I can tell him all about my –'

'Your scheme for creating money out of papyrus! He'll think you're insane!' interrupted Thethi.

'But it'll work. I know it will. After all, what would be the difference between those copper coins we use for loose change and a papyrus note? Just think about it, papyrus notes could hold any value we care to write on them. All it would take is for each one of them to contain a line saying something like the Pharaoh promises to pay the bearer the amount included in the note. That, backed-up by the option of swapping notes directly into some of the gold stored in the Pharaoh's pyramid bank, would do it.'

'Of course,' said Thethi rolling his eyes.

'I think *Promissory Notes* are your greatest idea, master' said Thoth.

'Promissory Notes? Yes that's what I called them. Thank you for reminding me, Thoth. Then there are the Financial Instruments. That's what I called them, didn't I, Thoth?'

'The what!' said Thethi.

'Financial Instruments, you know, the stocks and shares that I'm always discussing with Thoth.'

'No doubt written on more sheets of papyrus! Listen you two, do me a favour, try not to mention any of this until we order desert. I'd like to sample a few courses of the Pharaoh's cuisine before he kicks us out of the banqueting hall,' said Thethi.

'No, this is brilliant. No offence to you, Thoth, but we Egyptians will forget that we ever owned slaves if I can persuade Pharaoh to introduce Promissory Notes and their like. The EU will go from strength-to-strength and I might even be made Royal Chancellor.'

CHAPTER EIGHT

One seat remained unoccupied at the long dining table situated at the numerical centre of the banqueting hall. It was the largest and most magnificent of the chairs, constructed from a dark wood that Thethi and Merkha had never seen before. The walls of the hall were ablaze with colour, reflecting the sandstones and granites inset within the highest quality white limestone. To the right of the Pharaoh's vacant chair was sat the Royal Chancellor, to the left sat Pawah the High Priest. On the other side of the table was Thethi, to his left Merkha and to his right was their slave, Thoth.

Then, to a great fanfare, everybody rose from their seats and the Pharaoh Khufu entered the hall. When Khufu was comfortably seated, he nodded and everyone retook their places.

The meal got off to a tentative start, but tongues started to loosen after the downing of a few beakers of pomegranate wine. Everyone except the Pharaoh and the slave, Thoth, indulged in conversation. As for Thethi, he didn't seem the least bit concerned that he might be eating his last meal on the gods' earth.

Merkha was bursting to tell everyone his theories on papyrus money, stocks, bonds and the creation of a new financial trading system, but was just about managing to contain himself. He passed the time indulging in idle chatter with the Royal Chancellor, waiting until the moment that he could address the Pharaoh directly. He wanted to be sure that Pharaoh knew who would be responsible for transforming the economy after the departure of the slaves. But even though he was greatly distracted, trying to catch the Pharaoh's eye, he did think it odd that nobody mentioned the referendum.

Then, after about half an hour, Khufu raised his right

hand, just ever so slightly, and a hush filled the room.

'I don't understand why the gods would favour such a fool,' said Khufu as he looked across the table at Thethi. 'You are nothing more than a common drunkard. And yet the future of the Egyptian nation rests on the outcome of your referendum. You assured me that the Israelites wouldn't dare vote to leave, and yet you actively encouraged their doing so. Didn't you?'

'I'm sorry, Your Highness, but I don't understand your question,' said Thethi.

'Surely you have heard about the slogan paraded through the markets of Memphis and Thebes on the side of a camel?' asked Pawah?'

'Who hasn't?' replied Thethi.

'Informants under the employ of the viziers of each conurbation have reported that the slogan daubed on each side of that camel unduly influenced the vote. What do any of you know about the slogan and the camel?' asked Pawah.

'They were my words,' said Thoth.

'Who gave you permission to speak, slave?' said Pawah.

'With respect to his Highness and all present. You asked a question, I have answered it. The informants of the Vizier of Memphis must already have told you that it was I who led the camel through the local marketplaces.'

'And what of Thebes?'

'The camel was stolen from me. I can only assume that those who stole it took it there for their own purposes.'

'Stand up, slave!' ordered Pawah.

Thoth rose to his feet as instructed.

The Pharaoh nodded in the direction of the head of the Pharaonic Guard. It was the signal that the doors were to be opened and a group of beggars escorted into the great hall.

'That is the man I saw parading the camel through the market place,' said one of the beggars pointing at Thoth.

'What say the rest of you?' asked Pawah.

'He's the one,' came the reply in unison.

'My High Priest tells me that your name is Ineni,' said Khufu. 'Is that what the beggars who frequent the marketplaces know you as? Or do you go by another name, slave?' asked the Pharaoh.

'I am known to all as Thoth, Your Highness.'

The Pharaoh nodded, the beggars were escorted out of the hall and the members of the Pharaonic Guard standing closest to Thoth placed their hands over the hilts of their Khopeshs.

'Just to be clear, gentlemen, this is the first time I've heard my slave, Ineni, blaspheming in this way,' said Merkha.

'And whose idea was the referendum, yours or the fool sitting in front of me?' asked Pharaoh.

'It was mine,' said Thoth. 'I implanted the idea into the mind of Thethi when he was under the influence of pomegranate wine.'

'And from there it was implanted into mine ... a truly great undertaking. My High Priest tells me that you have not been mutilated in the manner of an Israelite. To what race of mankind do you belong?'

'My home is the land of the great river.'

'And what would you have me do with the Israelites, Thoth?'

'They voted to leave, why not just let them go?'

'Why not indeed?' replied Khufu.

'I know it's not my place to speak, but I think I might have a solution to the mess that we find ourselves in,' said Merkha.

'You! The lowest of scribes! Dare to suggest that you might provide his Highness with better advice than I, Royal Chancellor of the Union!' said the Chancellor, barely able to contain his rage.

'Just hear me out. I've got some brilliant ideas on how to restructure the –'

'Enough,' said Khufu before rising to his feet and leaving the banqueting hall.

Thethi, sensing trouble, managed to quaff the last of the pomegranate wine from his goblet before he, Merkha and Thoth were hauled from their chairs.

'The gods still shine on you, gentlemen. From this moment onwards you are under house arrest. But rest assured, his Highness won't hesitate to have you executed should we catch you in any further act of insubordination,' said Pawah as the three of them were dragged out of the hall to pleas of 'It wasn't me, it was them!' from Merkha, who was desperately trying to dissociate himself from Thethi and Thoth.

'What the hell is going on, Thoth?' asked Merkha, after the three of them had been locked inside of their palatial prison.

'I don't understand what you mean, master,' replied Thoth.

'I can't believe that you'd place Moses and his cronies above us. I can just about understand why you'd betray that fool,' said Merkha looking over at Thethi. 'But what I have done to deserve this? Haven't I treated you well? I can't seriously believe that you'd prefer to wander the deserts dodging the bloodthirsty Sandpeople when you're onto such a good thing here.'

'But I have no loyalty to the man called Moses or the elders of the Israelites. So why would I place their welfare above yours?'

'I don't know, that's what I'm hoping you're going to tell me.'

'Partly, it is because I am but a humble slave, but mainly it is because I am a living god and your pharaoh is only a man.'

'What, you a god! I'm sorry Thoth, but I think you might have started to descend down the same path as that drunken idiot,' said Merkha pointing at Thethi.

'Idiot am I? Well who's more fool, you or I?' said Thethi.

'From where I'm sitting I'd say it's safe to say that you two are,' said Merkha.

'And yet you own a slave that does very little work, whom you allow to use a name of one of our most revered gods. I might be drunk but you can't see the wood for the trees, my friend. Like Thoth told the Pharaoh, he's the one who thought-up the referendum, he's the one who manipulated the Pharaoh into sanctioning it and he's the one who thought-up the words of the slogan I wrote on the side of the camel. And you know what, my friend? I bet you he's the one who persuaded the elders to transport the thing to the street markets of Thebes.'

'Bloody hell, when you say it like that, it does sound a bit like the actions of a divine or malignant force,' said Merkha looking more than a little afraid of his less than trusty manservant. 'Well god or no god, what's the point of it all, Thoth?'

'Maybe I am but a pawn in a bigger game being played out by the god of all gods! This has the makings of a tale that will be retold for millennia, does it not?'

'Well I suppose that it does. But that depends largely on the outcome, does it not?'

'Maybe it will form the basis of a morality tale, encouraging men and women of future generations to do what is right and proper.'

'How so?'

'Can it be right to enslave people?'

'Well, no, I suppose it can't,' said Merkha.

'And what about giving them a vote to decide their fate and not honouring the outcome?'

'Well that doesn't sound right either.'

'And is it right for one man's opinion to usurp all others?'

'By that, I trust you're talking treason again.'

'Should not the law makers be elected by the people and act in accordance of what they deem to be right and proper? Do crowds not contain wisdom?'

'I don't know where you're going with this, Thoth. In a week from now the Israelites will leave here for good and I'm assuming that you're intending on leaving with them. After all, under your own definition of wisdom, aren't you obliged to adhere to the will of your own people?' said Merkha with a big grin on his face.

'But as I told you. I am not an Israelite, so I have no need to adhere to the wisdom of that particular crowd. All I will say is this. Failure to adhere to the will of the people spells disaster. No amount of bribery and cajoling will heal the deep wounds inflicted by such a wrong.'

CHAPTER NINE

A week passed and the Israelites were allowed safe passage into the desert. But, as Thoth predicted, Pharaoh reneged on his promise and he sent his troops to herd them back again. The rest, as they say, is history. And the tale of the Exodus has been seared into the mind of humankind ever since.

Now, in a land far to the north of modern-day Egypt, another people has voted to leave. They too are being bribed and cajoled into changing their minds because their modern-day rulers don't agree with the wisdom of their decision. The magicians and the oracles might be long gone, but their place has been taken by PR gurus and survey data. No seas will need to be parted to complete this story. But should the collective will of the people be thwarted, is it not conceivable that the final outcome will have unforeseen and unwanted consequences?

The business secrets of Pharaohs are no secret at all. All the empires have achieved greatness off the backs of slavery and fait currency. Who knows? Might we be living at the dawn of a new age - a world without slavery, where cryptocurrencies will allow the wealth of the nations will be distributed evenly?

What happened to Merkha, Thoth and Thethi? They were banished to the extreme north of Egypt. To a country named Macedonia. A land so far from Egypt, that the High Priest, Pawah, assured the Pharaoh that their influence would never be felt within the borders of the Union for all eternity.

Pawah might have been right about Merkha and Thethi. They lived to ripe old ages, with Merkha working hard whilst Thethi continued to while away his days drinking and thinking-up get rich quick schemes. As for Thoth? Well he truly was a god and returned to Egypt in 332 BC in the company of a man who would change the country forever.

ABOUT THE AUTHOR

JOSEPH BUSA was educated at Royal Holloway College, University of London, where he took a BSc in Chemistry before going on to study a PGCE in the teaching of science at the University of Southampton. He has had a variety of jobs but hopes that in the writing of books he has found his true vocation in life. He was born and lives in London.

BUSINESS SECRETS OF THE PHARAOHS

Printed in Great Britain
by Amazon